ONLY A FEW DAYS

TRUDY RATTER

This is a work of nonfiction.

Ordering Information:

BookTrail Agency
8838 Sleepy Hollow Rd.
Kansas City, MO 64114

Printed in the United States of America

Table of Contents

Only a few days. (Crab dance)

The sun was baking hot. Mirror like shadows playing across the sand.

Red fiddler crabs were doing their sideways dance. Two by four turn around and begin again.

Cracks of lightning filled the clear blue sky, hitting the sea and bouncing off again. A small crowd had gathered on the hilltop. Sounds of "OH" coming from the people.

Now and again a sea bird would swoop hoping to chance his luck on the dancing fiddlers. Drifts of fiddle music came from the still heavy air. Moving in time with two by four. As the crowd watched the lighting cast a purple march across the clear sky.

More fiddlers joined their brethren as each one formed a group of 8. Then all stopped as the fork hit the water, making the sea rise in a white sheet all ragged round it edge.

This time the crabs turned to face the sea. They bowed their pincers and began again. In and out, face your partner, lock your claws and round again.

Slowly the music changed, in time with the crabs, another flash of bright white light. The crabs turned to face the shore again to face the shore going into groups of 16. Joining and claws and sideways left then to the right.

They began to do the hokey cokey only waving their left pinners in the air.

One more flash of Neptune's fork reached across the sky. As one by one the fiddlers, gathered in long lines across the sky. Then one by one they went into the sea. As if nothing had happened.

Bath

If this were a cartoon everybody would be seeing green steam raising in great clouds above the camp. Everyone within a kilometre, would know there was something bad up ahead – as they would feel oh so sick, and try to hold their breath as long as possible.

Spring had sprung in the Rockies, rope lines had sprung up, as if by magic from the ground. Billy cans of sweet-smelling soap appeared, again as by magic.

As a massive fire was ablaze in the middle of the clearing, it was added to every few minutes by two very enthusiastic stokers, who took their job very seriously indeed.

One by one the women, took their clothes from the men, as one by one they stepped into the tub. A pourer throw hot water into and over the cowboys as a rag and soap were tossed at the men.

Ten green bottles began to be sung, by the new clean boss as each man got in and out of the tub. Sheets of snow-white linen were strung between the trees, so they could dress in clean clothes.

The local barber from the town, then began to do a roaring trade, charging two bits for a hair cut and a clean shave. All this for the annual dance, and buggy ride across the plains.

The older men and women had seen it all before, as they did the very same thing, when they were young and married the girl of their dreams.

Bella's Garden

Young Bella loved her garden. It was a place of quiet, the place she would go to, if she wanted to think-get away from the computer, mobile phones and other phones. Many a time she thought to get rid of her phones, then what would her boss do, everything would grind to a halt.

Bella's garden sang to her, like no other place on earth. There was colour for every season of the year. Her garden was never the same one day to the next.

Opening the curtains, Bella once again saw her garden in all its glory. Summer was turning into the burnt colours of Autumn.

She looked-something was different this morning she could put her finger on it. Humming she tripped on light feet down the stairs. Putting the kettle on as she passed on her way, to the back door. She opened it, only to go right back in again. Pulling her thick woolly over her head out she went again.

Everything looked the same from the kitchen-nothing was out of place, so she went back inside and got her breakfast. If you call it that? One of these diet shakes, which was meant to be every vitamin and mineral she would need for the day.

Fresh orange juice, straight from the fruit. So, it said on the carton and a bunch of green leaves. Rabbit food her Grandfather would have said. Bella believed in a health living. Grandfather would have though it a whole load of rubbish.

No messages on the computer, no missed calls meant she could take her time going into work. Her boss would be fine.

Putting her beaker down she wondered out into the early morning sunlight. What had she seen from her bedroom window?

Morning Pixie, she said as she reached the garden. There was next doors cat sniffing, nothing new in that. Her swing seat was there. Going further in she spoke to the plants as was her usual way.

So, she turned and made her way back. The cat was following, like he always did. Passing her swing seat, Bella caught sight of something. Why had she not seen this before?

The seat was covered in a carpet of red roses, from top to bottom. She stepped back looking in wonder. For the roses bought a message.

Happy Birthday sister, in yellow with blue flowers giving the card a boarder. Bella had forgotten about her birthday and had got the day off, as a reward for her hard work.

Big Words

The architect's ravioli made his eyelashes go the colour of coriander, as he played his harmonium and the fiddle played along. On the hob sat a poppadum, its wrinkles, slowly vibrating with the heat.

My sister's teacher held an ice cream as it dripped down both his moustache and his eye lash. As the pensioner carried on up the highway, cleaning his boots, as they hit the taxi being driven by a villain.

The comet fell to earth as the humped back whale swam into a scene of pandemonium. He caught a cowboy drinking a dram. The wolf was cooking himself a fry up of eggs and a skinned rabbit he found in the glen.

Down in the voe a thirsty raven, with a toothache heard splashes close, as the vinegar made him vomit. To make up to the operator he ate a sugared biscuit.

On a big yellow bus, a comment was made about what they saw in the ocean. As the geography element of the lesson about the voe took place.

A sight for soar eyes, made the man stamp and sored through the sky, a thing you could not make up if you tried.

Black

Black all around, where were the stars? Here should be at least one bright star. He saw nothing.

The eagle had landed a while back. All checks were done, even a rest had been scheduled in somewhere.

He was all dolled up in his spacesuit. The spaceship just hung in space

Slowly rolling in a circle. Thrusters hissing now and then.

The man started checked his oxygen was running. No, he was breathing. No stars – surly there had to be stars? He called his crewmates, to look. Are you drunk? Came a sharp retaught. Do you see little green men, came another reply?

He could not understand, what was wrong with his mates? All he asked was where were the stars?

Night after night for as long as he could remember he had lain on his back dreaming, what it would be like among the stars.

Now there was none. Disappointment filled his soul like it was eating him up from his core.

You alright mate, came a voice in his ear? He just drifted on the cable, there out in space. He could give no answers, he could not understand.

A far-off voice speaking in his head. He could do nothing but stare out at the black nothingness. How long he did not know. All he remembered was another white clad thing appearing out the hatch.

He thought he was lying on a soft white cloud looking up at the stars. Then this voice in his ear asked if he was still here. He moved his arm but said nothing. Why were there no stars? He kept asking himself, as his mates pulled him inside.

The black came then it was a warm feeling, filling his whole body. How long he was in this strange void he did not know.

Only when he woke he was in his bunk, dreaming of been among the stars.

Books

The black book lite up, there standing on its cover stood a strange shape.

Its pages were old, yellow like tissue paper, in the librarians gloved hands. She had to be incredibly careful, as each movement she made the paper would turn to dust.

Jumping back the book lite up again. When she jumped, she screamed at the top of her voice. She was sure there was another sitting on the book. Two or three other folks came rushing in, to see what the racket was about.

Bang, then the book shone yet again, this time so close it felt, like the roof was alive. Two forks of light hit the table, hitting the book. It shone again, showing its old picture on its crumpled paper.

Someone moved, the light went dead, when the bang came this time it was further away, everyone stood waiting for the strike. They began to relax.

Just as they began to breath again, the windows the table and book, shone in a yellow green hue. The girl saw the monster this it was still on the book. It had not moved. A sty fold sound came from her mouth.

This time one of them had the sense to light a lighter and went over to the book. She cried out. Getting a freezing look from her companion.

The table was bathed in a small light, just enough to show the books pages. Sounds of low crying could be heard as he looked down at the book.

It did not bother him that the bangs and cracks were further away now. He just grinned as he lifted the book up with gentle care.

What he saw made him happy. He showed everyone the picture of Winnie the Pooh and Piglet playing Pooh Sticks in the 100-acre wood.

It was a rare first addition of a very round honey licking bear.

Butterfly hart

A light breeze spreads over her soft young face.
Butterflies hang in the early evening air.
The buzz of a bumble bee gently alights on a sunflower.
A flutter of a happy hart as she looks, into the young man's eyes.
Her hart gives a gentle flip, as her hart gives a butterfly flutter.

All she can see is those soft brown eyes gazing into hers.
She looks onto his face and all she sees, is a love that swells,
Till her hart could burst with pride.

The love of a man is a wonderful thing to behold.
To feel his arms surround you with love.
His love reacts to make you feel safe. He is your world.

The love of a man is a wonder to behold.
To feel safe at last.
The love of a man is a dream come true.

Clock

There it was again. That infernal tick. It was somewhere in the room-but where? Tick, tock, the sound was going through Jessica's brain like a drum. What made it worse was the nagging voice in her head. Telling her to shut the thing up. That voice always, said or told her what to do. Why would it not stop giving her the jip?

Tock there it was again. Jessica put her hands over her ears, to block both sounds out. She begun to pull her hair, her long dark hair that fell down her back.

Finally, she began to get control. She was not going to be beaten not by a clock, or the ever-present voice in her head.

Tick, that was it. Enough, shouting out loud, she told the clock to "Shut the hell up" And voice you can also take a running jump, she said to the room.

Going over to the bookcase Jessica began to look. Taking out a book and putting her ears to the space, to see if the clock was near. No luck this time.

Tock it came from somewhere on her left and behind. For goodness sake, shut the thing up, said the voice in her head. Why don't you shut up she snarled at the voice?

If its to my left she thought, why not go over to the wall and begin there?

Tick, the clock was much louder now and nearer too. This time there was a tick, tock, tick. Jessica could almost feel it, the sound was so near. Your getting nearer, the voice said. Okay said Jessica, if your so clever, see if you can find it? She said to the voice.

Standing still she closed her eyes. Okay voice do your worst she again Jessica thought. Okay picture the room. She stood with her eyes shut, thinking what the room looked like.

Pictures on the wall the clock was not there. Windowsill, now that had a shelf. So, she looked. Just her cat napping.

Your warming said her voice. Once again Jessica stopped, what was next. Another picture and a mirror. Cross them off the list.

With a snap Jessica came to life. Her father's chair and his desk. She ran over, what a mess the desk was paper's books empty cups, even the remains of a sandwich.

Tick, tock it was here right in front of her. But where? Getting the basket, she throws the rubbish into it as fast as she could. Tick, tock she felt the table grown at the sound.

Jessica stopped. It was no good. Come on girl said the voice. Why stop now? She sat down in the chair. If it were a clock, where would I be, she thought. It had to be seen. She went around the desk and began looking under the mountains of paper.

Tick tock, tick tock, the bell was going off, making the paper move. Little by little, the clock face came into sight.

Their you are Jessica cried, hugging the clock. Stop it, stop it said the voice. NO, you stop it, cried Jessica, as the voice faded away. Her mind was quiet at last.

"Cooking Smells"

Everyone was staring across the road, noses where pointing up in the air, all the same way. Dreaming about the same thing. Smells intoxicating smells.

Cars were cashing into one another. No one seemed to notice all the devastation.

The smells were coming down the garden path, at a high rate of knots. Who ever it was, had just put a batch of cookies on the window sill.

Yet more cars were piling up in the street. Horns screaming at the tops of their voices. Fires were starting amongst the vehicles.

The trail to the house was getting longer. On one wanted to move. A gentle push was all it took, as first one then another began to move like dominos, knocking into one another. Everything went in slow motion.

No one could see where they were going. As their noses were still in the air.

This time an apple pie appeared at the window. Great clouds

Wafted through the air. The music changed from an English country garden, to great balls of fire. With one great crash, a steamed pudding appeared at the window. Overhead appeared out of the blue, a giant tin of custard. The music changed yet again, back to an English country garden.

As the custard poured into a dish with the apple pie in one small dish a cookie in the medium dish and the steam pudding was in a massive dish.

Then as the picture began to fade. A custard pie appeared across the screen ....

Corned Beef,

The kids rushed to the table, falling through the door all in a heap.

Teatime the gong had rung, cook had, watched with a warning eye, as each one pumped the water as cold as ice rushed into the butt.

Knocking chairs shouting at the tops of there voices. Everyone scraped into their chairs. The minister put up his hand, all fell quiet. A giggle there a cough that all that could be heard.

Cook came in, with a steaming bowl. One great groan escaped from the boys as they saw what it was. Not boiled beef. It was hard and tough as old nails. One mouthful would make their jaws ache.

Again, the big hand went up – as he stood and cast a stern eye over the table. Bid and braces were pulled up tiny hands wiped along the denim as the man said grace. None listened whispers could be heard from restless tongues as the boys began to fight. Amen boomed the voice, as everything became a wall of sound.

Cook pulled this way, that way at the lino like meat. As potatoes and carrots, gravy with great chunks of bread were handed out.

The boy's jaws began to ache as one by one, as the bits of beef became that lino in their small mouths. By this time cook had bought a pudding to the table. Not one child had finished his plate.

Steamed scilliy and dough was sending whiffs of apple and spice through the air, as one by one each plate would go under the table to let the hounds eat the beef.

Clever boys that they were, not one showed a sign of where the dreaded food went, as they ate with glee their scilly and dough.

Dancing Beams

As the glitterball goes round, a sunbeam hits the centre making
a long finger of shinning stars shine across the room.
The glowing beams hit the slippery floor, making the beams dance a merry dance.
Atop the shinning ball, light fairies trip the light fantastic making it glow a silvery glow.
As their light gossamer wings flutter and play with peels of joy and laugher.

The soft light movement of the fairy's feet make the ball jump with a playful laugh.
As the fairy feet, trip along the shiny slippery surface.
A rainbow of glimmering colour hits the fairy's wings as they play along the beams.
With kisses of sunlight the magic ball rolls around with happy delight.

As the rivers of light hit the dancer's floor, it darts up and down as
different shiny sharps are made, with the dancers' happy feet.
As merry peels of happy laughter echo through the star struck night.

D-Day

I was not there; I am not even anywhere near 70 years old. I have no idea what kind of hell, those poor men went through.

All I can do is think of pictures in my head. After reading a lot and watching films and old archive of the history of that time.

My stepfather trained on Slapton Sands, in Devon. Where my sister and her family live now. Slapton is a 3-mile-long flat beach, with a café and a couple of houses at its end. At least it was when I was last there some 10 years ago now. It is a single-track road. With a freshwater lake on the other side the track.

Although my stepfather never spoke of it much. That is what made me more interested in WW2. To learn more whatever side, you were on. To top that my birth father was also in the war. He was a member of the Black Watch, so when I was young, he was always away on different missions. I did not find out till just before he died that he was undercover, for most of the war. He came away with 4 medals.

My step dad was a cover for Montgomery, as he was the spitting image of the man. I even saw a couple of photos of them both together. When they were both in Africa on campaign.

Before that he was among the many who helped take back Rome. Even though it was the United States that got the credit for that one.

All week there had been programmes of remembrance on the TV about D-Day. With re-enactments of the beach invasions.

I am not sure I like the idea of re-enactments. As the veterans are getting smaller by the day. You see pictures of them grouped together with tears in their eyes, remembering, the day they went to war.

Fiddlers Folly

Jasmin's folly stood at the very point of the station. Fiddlers village was at the bottom of a very steep hill. So steep it needed its own train station. I say station, to look at it, it was nothing of the sort. Just a single car at each end going up and down on a very thin wire.

The Folly was on the very edge of a steep crumbly cliff, of very bright white chalk.

Fiddlers folk were enormously proud of the little building, which from down below looked like, it stood in mid-air, moving on a cloud of cotton wool.

The villagers had carted every shell, rock and pieces of wood, up to the point of the hill – way before the railway was a twinkle in anyone's eye.

It had been an idea of one of the villager's back then, to give something to do for the young ones, who's fathers and brothers had gone to war.

At that time, the village was a sleepy place, right on the edge of the Scottish mainland. A place that time really had forgotten. The folk had their own ways and laws, folk married into families who were part of the village.

Everyone walked or rode the odd horse. A car or bike were unheard of. They could get the radio, but only on calm days. Fiddlers would have gone on its own slow exitance. If the planes and ships had not sailed past, on their way up to Orkney. So, a couple of men decided to walk down to the next village, a day's walk away.

From then on Fiddlers slept no more. Whether they were young or old. The men folk wanted to do their bit. So, apart from women and children, the odd old person, there was no life in the once calm village.

They built homes, built masts so they could get the radio, whatever the weather.

Then the folly was born, one night in the local pub. The children were sullen, weak and quiet – no more laughter fun or games.

Nights of roaring fires, pints of ale were downed in the planning of the folly. Folks offered horses, buckets, what ever it took, to bring the children alive again, they would get it done.

What happened next took everyone by surprise. A ship anchored in the bay, way down in the valley. But what went on you will have to wait, until another bedtime story.........

Figures

The mist lay incredibly low on the ground, finger lengths along its edge.

The dog stopped, running back behind his master. The man looked down, he had never seen Jeb, act like this before. The Blood hound was a great hunter, even with ears going along the muddy path.

The hunter looked ahead, even with the great 12 bore ready by his side. One shot from the great beast and nothing would be left.

He thought or was it just a glimpse of something crossing his path? The dog went tighter into his master's leg. Hunter blinked there it was again. Clear this time, he thought he caught a glimpse of a black cape – but was unsure yet again.

The hound suddenly gave one of his baying howls. It must be a convict from the jail? The byu was doing strange things, the mist was hanging on the trees, like a spider's web. By this time, the carpet had become a thick cotton sheet.

His hound stood and raced back, the way they had come. A sharp whistle carried across the cold air. The hairs went up on the hunter's neck. He shivered. He thought he was been a silly old fool. He knew the byu, like the back of his hand. He even walked them in the dark.

Even he was getting spooked now. His dog came racing back, this time running into the trees. The hunter had, had enough he was not scared of ghosts. There was no such thing.

Reading his 12 bore, he disappeared into the byu never to be seen again.

Fire

How I miss my open fire. I would sit watching those bright licking flames.

My father-in-law taut me how to lay a fire, with peat and a firelighter. I became so good at it, the old folk would ask me to get the fire going from the embers, of the night before. Then I would sit and watch the flame burning through the peat.

I often wondered, that if in another life, I was a fire raiser. To see a volcano at night – is a thing of beauty to me. I know they can be deadly, but there is an odd peace that comes over me, when I see that molten heat slowly go across the countryside.

Oh, how I miss my open fire. Now with the modern heating, there is not a soft gentle heat, just a harsh dry air, that stifles, every breath I take.

What is it that the sight of a fire does to calm my ragged nerves? To look at the flames, I do not see demons or the devil, within the white-hot flames. Just a calming gentle heat.

To see a log fire and hear the crackle of the logs as they burn, it makes me warm inside. I remember when I was young, how the grown ups would toast, bread and crumpets, using a long toasting fork, how good they would be.

To see my Gran's old kettle all covered in black soot and sing that the water was ready. Those happy memories of the good old days when I had no worries.

How happy I would be now, in my old age, to see an open fire, I would sit in a rocking chair, knit and watch those fiery flames.

Flag

The flag lay raged wet and lonely. The soldiers stood around not really knowing what to do. Should they leave the flag on the ground and pretend they had not found it? They lived by its code. Gold with a ring of laurel leaves, its flagpole was 6 feet high.

This flag was different, it had no edge. No leaves. Instead it was blue, with a stone hammer in one corner. The men had no idea who it belonged to. They were just home to a nice warm flaggen and just maybe a wench or two.

The Generals horse on seeing this thing on the cobbles reared and sent the General flying. Landing in the mud, his red cap no longer red.

A few giggles came up from the ranks, only to get a cold dark stare, from the man on the ground. One or two went to help the sodden man to his feet. Others ran after the bolting horse.

A young lad who waited on the "big man," saw the flag. It was heavy and still on its pole. The boy pulled, till he could pull no more. A soldier to his left took pity on the boy and rose the heavy flagpole and all into the air. Then with great strength planted it into the ground at the edge of the road.

The General now standing. Came over to look at the strange piece of cloth. It was once as dark as the night sky. He could just see the stars, embroidered with thread, against the sky. In the corner was the great hammer. Which was done with white thread. The hammer looked like it was going to hit something, that was not there.

The General turned looked at his man who had set in the ground. Take the flag off the pole – and carry it back. Then turned not even giving the man a nod of thanks.

Boy – wine said the General – as a second thought to the boy who scuttled off at top speed. Some while later his horse was bought back. A little worse for wear.

Slowly with their new prize the romans returned to barracks, wondering what tails this flag could tell ....

Food

I dream of ice-cream, cakes of vanilla, strawberry boats with green threads of grass for its oars.

Here sitting in the strawberry bough, sits a pale nut-brown field

Mouse. With whiskers of pale straw.

If you listen, he is whistling a happy little tune. Tapping his feet in

time with his song. Down on the riverbank, out comes Ratty, looks up, as a huge rain drop, drops on his velvet nose.

With its scream and cry, everyone looks up, as the crow, drives head long into the long grass now been soaked by the light shower.

Up pops a rainbow as the shower crosses the sunlight. Landing just out of reach. Not showing its pot of gold.

In my dream, I walk alone among the blue bells, soft under my bare feet, feeling the warm breeze touching my face. Butterflies fly around like soft lace.

Bare moss lies like a curtain, as I dream.

Then slowly as the dream I awake warm and snug beneath my quilt.

Fourteen Saints

Around the table just as King Arthur did with his Knights of old sat fourteen Saints.

Most were praying, some were chatting.

St. Therese of Lisieux, stood asking for quiet.

"Oh, men of peace and good will" hear me.

All went quiet, "Here we sit", sitting and looking down

On this fragile earth, we call home.

St. Patrick of Ireland rose to his feet and spoke.

"This world that we knew is now a very different place"

No more do the people ask us for our help. Instead they fight amongst themselves. Now their land on which they live, is a quite different place, full of illness killing its people.

Pope St. John Paul II spoke in his quiet gentle tones.

"It is time to prey that this once loving world now full of disease and war, be bought back to peace and harmony."

So, one by one, they chose to kneel in the Garden of Peace, and pray to the Father for help to heel this war torn sick struggling brave world.

Heal this troubled world

Fire, famine and illness cover the land and seven seas.
The fire rages in the natural wild forest,
Animals, birds and the fish in the sea, run or flee for their lives.
Some never make it out in time to live wild and free.
Please let this world heal.

The grounds left dark and grey,
No fresh water, its all gone dried by the fearsome heat.
Nothing for human or animals to eat.
Lord on high, please let the world heal.

Plague covers the land and sea; it knows no boarder or boundaries.
My Lord on high, let your stricken people breath.
All to live and bless you for another day.

HillWalkers

The hill was wet – soaking wet. The hard hats were doing their best to take the hill. Hill of Hell was its nick name. Mile after endless mile – hour after hour the men were wiry, but still they kept coming.

The men had gone deaf to the noise, awhile back. They never even noticed when a marine went down his life ripped away.

The sand was no more, all it was just a mass of human flesh. Be it whole or bits.

One man got his eyes on the great gun, blazing every few minutes. Nothing mattered, he just had to get to that gun.

First to his right then to his left. He was the ship that had taken him and many others across to a strange land. First one way then another all he could see was the gun, peeping out its bunker.

Days of sorrow would be felt later in years to come – when he and others would be long gone defending their homeland. No matter what colour, or who they would worship.

He would never the fields of Flanders, all a sea of Blood Red Poppies. All he could see was this tongue of fire, burning and scorching everything in its path.

Like so many he was almost at the top, and like many before, he did not know his end. He just knew he had almost reached his goal.

We will remember them.

If only I could ....

Rain, wind, fire and snow he had seen it all. Had even been there through two World Wars. Trapped in his own confined space. For so long he was at peace of joy and quiet. He felt safe, as no one knew he was there. He could look out listen to the people passing by or even standing beside him.

Pigeons used him as a perch. He did not worry about all the mess that the birds left behind. Such was life.

Fashions came and went. It was interesting to see how much or even how little the ladies wore now. Even the men wore some odd things. Long chains coming out from their noses, wrapped around their waist. He used to be in those chains, – his wrists in big thick iron – even his feet were surrounded by the rough iron rings. The men of this new world, used to whip, their bodies opening them up to the warm flow of fresh blood. Their backs covered in scars old and new.

They would be called everything under the sun, but never their God given name. N..... or B.. was what came forth. Many of his fellow human beings, for that's what they were. Could not understand a word these cruel people said.

It did not take long, to learn that if they complied stopped responding. They were not wiped and shouted at but treated like the human beings they were.

Each family if that is what they were was given a hut with a dry roof over their head. A place where they could rest, cook, grow food and sleep in safety, without fear.

Many would go to church on Sunday and sing their joyful harts out.

In the last few days things had changed around about his silent world.

It had been so peaceful and quiet with just the birds

It is heavy

What is it that makes it pop up when you do not expect it?

Your hart weighs as heavy as an elephant, with dreed.

The blood moves fast through your body, as your hart beats at 100 beats a minute.

So much so it makes you head light, as if to faint.

Then through the dark mists of hell, you see a path.

It twists and turns; it goes back on itself.

It makes you drop to the ground, with what feels the weight of two men.

It is heavy.

As you walk out of the mist your eyes can see as you slowly walk into the light, a joy you never knew could happen.

Joyful Harvest

Bright orange, green and maybe white they sit there.
Joined by a dark green with a hint of red cabbage they
Sit there.
A corn dolly joins the harvest and sits atop the largest
Orange pumpkin.

Sweet shinning apples all red with blush, sit proudly
Amongst the strew fresh in from the fields.
Carrots dirt still caked over them, are guarding the parsnips
All creamy and white.

As the church opens its doors the people are welcomed
In from the cold Autumn chill.
Each with a candle in a gloved hand presenting them
Gifts of harvest home all proud and given with love.
Then sit with grace as the gift from God of another harvest
Bought in.
Thankful for a harvest to see them through the cold and snow.

Knitting

Click, clickity, click the needles were going so fast, you could not see the knitting, pass over her needles, but it was growing all the same.

Her TV was on, with one of the weekly soaps beginning its next crises. All in one sad half hour. It was just so unreal. The women took on notice, she just stared ahead but still her knitting grow.

Outside the wind howled, as it went around the house. The curtains blow gently, as a draft came through the windows. The woman changed her yarn, weaving it in and out. Where slowly a picture grows as the knitting got longer.

The programme changed, a film came on, and sorry music began to fill the air – but still the woman stared ahead as the knitting grow.

With a loud crash the door blows open, sending a cold blast of air into the room. No blink, the women went on knitting and it grow.

Her cat came in, in its rush its fur springing from its body, making it look like it had, had an electric shock and still the knitting grow.

Another change as the clock in the corner chimed its hour. The news came booming out of the TV, as the knitting snaked its way to the floor.

The dark came down, and the only light came from the open fire. The woman stopped knitting and throw a peat or two onto the fire. The cat now washing itself on the mat, decided to play with the wool. No matter the woman just knitted away as it touched the floor.

As the TV man said goodnight, the women stopped and looked up. Still the breeze blow as the curtains moved. Whistling through the gaps.

The women stood, put her knitting in the basket, lay the fire to rest and shut the door. The TV went off as the women faded in the air. Then once again the women could be seen with the TV on and slowly the knitting grow.

Letter of wishes, what do I write?

Toby sat looking at his laptop. It had to be now or never. He had been putting the letter off for weeks now. He had been staring at the bubbles for awhile clicking the mouse now and again. His Dad had asked him to write to his old friend.

His Dad was not able to do so anymore, mores the shame he thought, after all Ted was his old buddy.

Dad had finally given in, to his failing body. His mind was still there, he could still speak slowly. He had been living with his son, for a couple of years.

Since his Mother had passed away. She had been his career, friend, lover for well over 50 years. They just had to look at each other to know what the other was thinking.

His Dad had made up his mind – if he was going into the Nursing Home, then he wanted to make a clean break – from everything and everyone. Neither Toby nor his wife liked the idea, but it was his father's wish.

The trouble was how do you tell a friend, you had known from childhood, to just go away out of his life? Because his father did not want his dear friend to see him like this. It just was not done.

Toby sat thinking of all the good times they had. Fishing for tiddlers off a rickety old bridge. Even jumping in puddles as the rain came bucketing down. The rain going into his brand-new wellies.

Or the day of the carol concert, one snow covered day. His Dad coming to the rescue when the school lights gave out.

A tear fell on the laptop. Bringing Toby out of his thoughts. He thought about writing to the old man, instead of typing, but that would never solve the problem.

His wife came in, with a cup of tea, looked at him, placed a gentle hand, on his shoulder, and went out.

Toby began to type.

Dear Ted,

This is not going to be easy, however I am writing on behalf of my Dad.

He has decided to go into a Nursing Home.

Was how Toby began his letter, with tears welling up in his eyes.

It was now or never ....

Lonely Playground

Up and down, up and down went the see saw, empty now,

As the light breeze moves it slowly.

The breeze makes the child's swing as it slowly goes back and forth.

The slide shines as the rain drops begin to roll down its slope.

A bird sits on the roundabout as it squeaks in its roundabout ways,

Not beginning never ending.

A balloon drifts by on the gentle breeze.

As one by one the children come back, after the light spring shower.

Love is forever.

One starry night, when the sky was clear and the Aurora was filling the night sky with it soft gentle sound.

A North Star, and A Western Star crossed each other's paths. Somehow while the Aurora sang, they crossed many times over.

On the Western stars final approach, he stopped drawn by he knew not what. Down from the North the other star stopped. Their starry tails touching oh ever so gently.

Over the course of time even though the Aurora stopped her song. The two lovers gave up their hearts, over the course of many years, only blink in our eyes but a millennium to them. Their starry tails become one.

Until in the blink of our eyes a Love was born, which will last forever.

Maggie Sat.

The rocking chair creaked, it needed oiling, but old Maggie did not bother – old well worn in the face she just rocked in her chair.

The other people in the room, although around her age, just stared ahead as if in a dream. Not Maggie her mind was all there. Maggie was with it alright.

What let her down was her body. The nurse came in. Oh, here she comes with her baby ways, thought Maggie. Oh, how she would love to shout out load. So, they could know what Maggie thought Certainly, no little old lady – with grey curly hair.

To cover her annoyance, she took up her knitting. How fast those knitting needles moved, in a real blur.

Here Maggie said the nurse, shoving a drinking cup in her face. Maybe if she gave her a look, Maggie might be able to give the other women a hint. If looks could kill thought Maggie.

Then it happened out of the blue, the cup went flying across the room. The top coming off the mug and its contents soaking the old man, next to her.

The nurse shouted at Maggie racing towards the old man. Yes, yes, yes thought the old woman. I will show them, with a wicked grin spreading all over her face.

Maggie, shouted another nurse, crashing through the door. Boy was she pleased, Jim might be wet, but it meant things were coming to life now.

Jim got whisked away, no doubt to be dried off. Maggie felt young again. Her body might not be okay her will, but her thoughts were still as crisp as when she was young.

Oh, yes, they would complain to her son, he would agree nod his head and just smile. He would know his Mother was okay.

Magic Windows

Little bright beams shine on the magic windows.

So the sun shows its happy face.

Sometimes it is the light from inside and in us that shines on the magic windows.

On windows of beauty, how we miss your happy face.

both seem to smile as we go through the door, as they welcome us in.

One in front one behind another single one, guarding this happy place.

How warm your greeting is when we step inside the door.

Joy will be the time when we sing to you again.

More haste, less speed

Rush, work, rush that 's all it was, trying to get one thing done. All my body was trying to tell me "Slow Down" but would I no way.

All it was, was a passport photograph. The information on the screen kept saying Not readable – not clear enough. It did not help that my hands would NOT help, I cannot text on my phone, because of the shakes.

It did not help that; the photo might end up in something good for me. No, I still had to plough into it and get the thing taken.

My head ached, with voices left and right hammering at my ears. At one stage I could have banged my head into a wall. Which has happened a few times in the past. Not that it would have done the wall or me any good.

I did not eat for hours, missed my meds time – missed my meds time – but still a stubborn voice inside said, "Keep going".

I still must get the photo done, but this time I will have help. I hope? I am stubborn to my own helplessness.

Slowly, oh, so slowly I am learning to seek out that help. Lockdown does not help, when only one or two people can come into the house.

Today is another day. If the photo gets done it will. If not, it can wait another day. Today is for me, my family and a gentle bouncing dog.

Mystery Hut

The wind was raging outside, down by the hut they had found for the night.

The young campers were feeling somewhat cold, for they had not been able to light a fire. So, they huddled together to keep themselves warm.

The hut shook each time the wind gusted around the wobbly walls. Making them think the hut would grow wings and take off, into the night. Dawn began to raise, with the wind still battering the fragile hut – but still it stood.

Once day light came up, they decided to get out of their wet clothes. Their shyness just went out the window. They hurriedly dug into their rucksacks, to find something dry to wear.

There was an open fireplace, up by the back wall. Already to be lite. Which the young folk had missed as they piled into the door.

Across its mantle hung a light rope line. As they got warm and found more firewood and peat, the hut began to warm, leaving a cheery glow along the wooden walls.

Their wet clothes were steaming as they dried in front of the fire. They found an old kettle, and filled it with rainwater, dripping from the door.

Full up now with hot food and thick dark coffee, they began to plan, what to do next. The rain was still coming down, but the gale was just a whisper with an eery cheery sound. They thought it better to stay where they were that day.

So, board games, cards even the odd book made its way into the grey daylight. Even the diary was added to about the mystery hut, sitting by the open fire.

Another night came and went, with the day dawning calm and bright. So, they packed their things and ventured out the door.

How lovely a sight, was to behold, as they gazed upon the lough. Colours of purple heather, greens of every shade. With a dark brown tree like bush dotted along the shore.

There just off to the left of the hut, was another outdoor line. They looked at each other, back to the line. To see three divers' suits, hanging all in ribbons.

One small the next was middle size with an adult one hanging on the end. How long they had been hanging on the line, the young ones could not guess?

Chatting they looked at the suits, and carefully took them down. Their names were in each one. Carrie, Dan and Bill. On careful study they found inside a hidden ankle pocket a newspaper clipping, with a photo of the wetsuit people, all in happier times. On the clipping could be seen the date up in the corner. August 1999.

Why did they leave their wetsuits there hanging on the line? Only those three wetsuits knew, but the story would never be told.

Noise

Belt up, she wanted to shout, as many voices rose in one loud shout.

These voices going round in her head. Just wanted to get out and beat the noise right down.

Belt up the old women, thought as the ladies came round with her tea. Once more her arm flew out, this time Jim just ducked as the now flying cup, reached its hight.

With a look of glee upon Maggie's face she just sat and enjoyed the scene.

Oh, gentle breeze

Gentle is the breeze, that blows the leaves.
That watery sunshine that plays on the water's edge
Sea foam playing along the roaming tide way.

Quiet water with a gentle ripple, as a crab or two
Slowly make their way up the golden beach.

Up on the road a car slowly makes its way across the leaf covered
Road.
Orange, yellow, green, red and light brown,
Cover the dark damp tarmac road.

A rabbit, looking for a bite to eat, stops
As a leaf, drifts in front of him.
The cat laying in the undergrowth, watches
The young animal as he cleans his whiskers.

Gentle is the breeze as it waves across the bay.

One, two, three

One, two, three Ruben's eyes glowed, a mean dark glance. Swish snap the whip crashed above the man's head. Robin was different, Ruben's twin not a bit like his brother. Robin was quiet – he hated his father waving the hide whip.

Go on Dad called Ruben at the side of the ring. He was every bit as mean as he looked. Those green eyes shown like jewels.

Robin thought he could see the lion's eyes blink with fear. He wanted to tell his father to stop and Ruben to shut up – but he was just too quiet to say anything out loud.

The boys were born into the circus. From an early age Ruben was always the mean one. Kicking, punching. He would even break his brother's toys.

Robin hated the circus, everything about it. The worse was seeing the animals – being made to do tricks and fear in their eyes. Elephants were caned, lions and tigers whipped all so people could laugh and glare at them.

Robin could not even kill as fly. One day he caught Ruben pinning a dragonfly upon the caravan wall. Robin came off the worse for ware in that fight. He ended up with a spilt lip and a broken nose. Just because he tried to save the dragonfly.

Their father called the boys, to come into the ring. Robin froze. Ruben could not get there quick enough. Pulling the whip out of his fathers' hand. The whip sang through the air. One lion reared and jumped off his stool. The other hands quickly grabbed the boy kicking and screaming away from the scene. Ruben wanted the whip and tried to lash out, as the animals were guided back into their cages.

All this time Robin had been sitting on a seat at the side of the ring, tears rolling down his face. How he wished the lions could be free? There and then he made up his mind, that the circus life was not for him. He began to hatch a plan – he was going to run away.

The lion act did not appear that night. The circus owner felt it was too much of a risk.

Ruben was band from the tent for a whole month. So, he ended up taking it out on his brother, by kicking him out of the caravan. It was only after the show, when was found cold and shivering behind the "Big" tent.

What happened next, we will have to wait and see?

Outer space

Zagon, that mad bad green scaley person, who ruled the black beyond. How I hate him, my little brother, would get the comic book, week after boring week.

I could bet what little pocket money I had. Edward would be playing the latest story out. He had a 7th birthday party and all – I mean all his presents were about his world of Metlaw or Zargon himself. To make it worse I was the only girl and I am 11. So boring.

Next time our changed his bed. There was Zargon, his face screaming from the quilt cover.

Not long after that, Edward had a room change. He was now in the land of Metlaw. The whole room was looking like the dark side of the moon.

Edward came to find me one day. Came charging in and rushed out again screaming at the top of his voice. Younger brothers do not like Boy Band's. Got him!!!

Peace Brakes

Peace is the heart of our soul.

Peace is in every twist and turn of our being.

Light and dark, the light is the happiness flowing

Through our blood, where the dark is our very thought

In the darkest reaches of our mind.

Peace will come from the smallest thing, a chink of

Dappled sun light or something that someone has said.

Peace can be seen in the light of a child's eye gazing up to

Its parents' or of a mare just given birth to it new foal.

Peace is a state of mind that brings joy to all that takes it in.

Playing ball

The pitter patter of rain drops, echoed as the child entered the tunnel. His little shoed foot steps echoing around the walls. His shinny new blue shoes making a clipping sound as he ran.

He ran as fast as his little feet would carry him after his little blue ball. He was pulling a little wooden train behind him as it clattered along the concrete floor.

Shuts of David could be heard as his big sister ran after him. The ball rolled into the sun light, and came to a light jumping halt, against an old oil drum.

Puffing and out of breath, David came to a halt, beside his way would ball. With giggles of pure joy, the little boy. Picked up his ball, turned round and throw the little blue ball back down the tunnel, and giggling ran after it again.

Prison

The day was beginning as every other day, in the past two years. He waited till the knock on the door came from the other side. After that he had 15 minutes to wash, dress and make his bed.

When

the first door banged open, he had to race to his window. Standing bolt upright, arms by his side. He dare not make a move. How he longed to be free of this grey dark dungeon of a place.

Crash, he came out of his dream with a jump. 678 ready sir he shouted, as the Officer came in. One at the door, another going through his shelves, looking under his bed and turning the neat bedding into a shambles.

He could do nothing but watch, as the Officer at the door, stared into his eyes. He began to clench his fists, the Office moved, and he relaxed, he knew it would only provoke the man and nothing was going to stop him getting out in a couple of days.

He could not say, it had changed him, been behind bars. Okay he did as he was told, they all did just like a robot.

For two years his day had been an order, when to eat, drink, work or even exercise around the yard. Even when to sleep. In two days, all this would change. Truth was he was scared down to his boots. He liked to have his life in order. He did not want to go out into the big wide world.

It was from that moment he began to think of a plan. Freedom, it was not what everyone thought it was.

Quiet

Still are the leaves, as the blossom covers the cherry tree. A squirrel runs along a newly leafed branch, when the snow-white blossom floats gently down.

Down below, stands a fallow deer, as the blossom falls on its nose. His ears go up, all alert. He stamps his foot. Then as he settles, and nothing happens, he starts to eat again.

The cherry tree stands by a babbling brook, its water gently running across the pebbled shore. Out jumps a trout, its shiny silver skin shinning and dancing in the sunlight.

Down swoops a Kingfisher, blue green shafts of light going across his arrow like shape.

Out pops a harvest mouse, from among the field of yellow flowers. Then sits and washes its whiskers.

As the song thrush of its joy at the lovely day. Its like time stands still, as the last pieces of the puzzle are put into place.

Rain Drops

Little Roy stood, by the window all 2 foot 5 inches of him.

The day was cold, with a wild wind blowing. The rain, like hard hail, hitting the sitting room window.

Small stubby fingers traced the rain down the long, tall window pain. Roy's big yellow digger sat sadly in the middle of the lawn. Its digger arm was up, as the rain was filling the bucket as fast as it could. Till his little bucket was overflowing.

Roy never knew he was been watched, his Grandfather had gone into the room and saw Roy by the window.

The man sat down saying nothing – he just watched his Grandson. How his little finger touched the glass and slowly traced it down following the water. How his little body shock with laughter as he chased the rain drops.

Roy spotted the dog, outside shaking himself, with a fountain of water spraying everywhere. Roy watched his pal racing about the garden rubbing up against the fence, because he was so wet. Yet moor giggles, as the dog jumped into a puddle.

Then while his Grandfather watched, the little boy's mood changed be began to cry. Red hot tears. His Grandfather went up to the little boy – and took him in his arms.

The man looked out the window, to see what had destressed the little boy.

All he could see was the sun coming out, and a rainbow spreading across the blue and white sky.

Reading

Once I read everyday. Now show me a book and I feel like throwing it across that crowed room. If there is any noise at all, even if a pin drop. My eardrum beats a thousand beats a minute. I could pass out.

I thought I might take a romance up and settle into all that mush. Not a chance those books are unreal. No sense to them what's so ever.

Instead I find myself, looking out the window, at people passing by. I began to dream about what people might do. Like the young boy, swinging on the swing turns into an aeroplane and he flies across the sky.

As I walk to my safe place, I can hear my voice calling me. I walk through the rose garden, and in the middle standing alone is a fountain. It drew me to it like a magnet. My voice is the water, sometimes slow sometimes it rages like a torrent, cashing down on the rocks from far above.

If I laugh, it leads me to another place. With wild raging fires. I hate to hear my own voice. I go to my quiet place then. I lie on the grass, with the sun on my face and watch the clouds in the sky forming up as animals two by two.

Then they begin to sing a gentle sound, calming me as I look out the window and dream.

Rock

That black rock, that is Foula, gave a massive stare, at the men as they rowed towards her. The lady was in one of her menacing moods.

Dark January days, with sharp sleet hitting both men and rock. It was their first fishing run after Christmas. The men were dressed in new ganseys, socks and caps.

When they first went out, the sky was still, not a cloud could be seen. So, the skipper decided to row for Foula, where he knew a fish or two could be found.

Fishing with line and many barred hocks, a good catch was made. The sixareen began to list to one side as the fish came aboard. Thinking they should turn for home; they turned the boat around and found their way back. As they rounded Foula the wind hit them from the side almost turning the sleek craft over.

Digging deep, heads down the men began to pull the oars, as they battled the wild wind. It did not help that the sleet on their faces. No amount of whisked skin could stop those needle-like stones.

Just as Papa came in sight – the wind changed its mood again and it drooped, with the sea like a mirror.

They knew they only had a matter of minutes before the winds anger would return twice as strong.

As they would always do, a fisher's wife would stand on the hilltop looking for the men. A small dark spot could be seen on the horizon. By now the dark mood was like a black cap covering all in sight.

The oil lamps appeared on the hilltop, as the boat gave one last push towards hame. As the women folk watched from way up high, the boat upended and lost everyone and everything on board. Never to be seen again.

Sacred book of books

Happy book, sorry book, nice book, book of joy and many tales
From Genesis to Malachi, from Matthew to Revelations.
A book of two books all in one. Within these books are many a story,
Waiting to be read.
This book we grow to love as we were growing up. We learn
through pictures and of the spoken word.

A guidebook and one of great knowledge. This great and wonderous book, is a joy to behold.
It can be of many languages and of faiths.
Whoever we might pray to and worship it is our guide throughout our life.
O great book of all books, a wonder to behold.

Sailboat

Little sailboat, sailing across the deep blue sea.

Gulls calling on the wind, watching the boat sail across out to the sea.

Sparkling diamonds piece the sunlight, as the boat goes on its way.

Painted sails catch the wind, as slowly the spin drift catches a wave.

Still the boat goes along its way, way out to sea the sailboat goes.

Slowly bobbing up and down.

In its wheelhouse stands a wooden man, painted hair of faded yellow.

A half-broken pipe breaks his mouth of rusted brown.

He holds the wheel with a steel like grace, just staring out to sea.

The sailboat slowly bobbing up and down, as it goes on its way.

Saying Goodbye

Done is the summer, it's gone to sleep for another year.

Gone are the bird song, of spring and summer,

Leaves falling off the trees, looking bare and dead.

Old father time does not stop – not even for the birds.

Gone is the cry of the seagulls flying overhead

Their rawcus scream silent till next year.

Dormice, hedgehogs' things of the glen bed down

Underground, to see out the cold winter months,

All cosy in their den.

Out come the hares, in their beautiful snow-white coat.

There goes a peasant, running for its life

As the hungry fox picks up speed.

Down swoops an angry eagle, as it catches a trout unawares.

Up comes the wind, as it blows the waves over the shore.

An earie song, as the wind picks up more strength.

Snow filled squeals as the wind gains yet more venom.

Then those heady days of winter sun. To make us smile again.

September – into December

September where had the year gone? July came and went. August was gone in a flash.

Now September, it seems like it. Ronny went to bed last night; the leaves were gently falling off the trees – in no hurry at all.

Then his alarm went off at 6a m. As usual, he went to the window – throw back the curtains, in great haste.

What the ..... he said out loud to no one in particular. As the cat went and rubbed its way against his legs

He gazed at his calendar after going downstairs. Yes, it was September. He pinched himself. No, it was no dream. Ronny tried his mobile. No signal. That was wrong. He lived right in the centre of town. He went over to his house phone, he picked that up. Nothing just silence met his ear.

The cat made itself known by clawing his leg. Jumping he remembered they both needed breakfast.

Dreaming he put cat food in his cereal bowl and cornflakes, in the cat's dish. Not even noticing his leg felt warm, looking down, he only then noticed the trickle of blood. Taking the towel, he dried his ragged leg.

Once more he went to the window. Yes it was still there. No dream. He tried his phone again. The answer was the same – nothing. It was the same when he tried his TV and radio station. This would not do. How was he expected to get to work? He had so much to do.

Instead here he was wondering how he was going to get out the door. This time when he saw the cat come by, he shouted at it. Startled the animal ran and hid under the table.

Looking at the clock, it was already 8a.m. He should have been on the road by now. Walking his way to work.

Instead he was staring at a different world, one he hated with all his might. In the night there had been a light shower of snow-white flakes, which had turned everything into a soft white carpet.

A wonderful scene. But not Ronny, he was a towny through and through. Towns never ever saw snow.

Silly rat.

The big brown rat, sat on a chair of mouldy blue cheese, surrounded by a cloudy green mist making its way to the roof.

Brown bear got an apple which got stuck on his claw and tired to bite it off. But instead he bit his paw and jumped right into the air.

A yellow ripe banana was what the chimp liked to eat only another one came and stole his lovely fruit and left him with the skin.

A steaming hot tart, lay on the windowsill, down came a bird, to take the tart away. Not knowing a trap lay in wait, as the bird pulled the tart, down came an axe and chopped off its head.

Silly Stuff

The squirrel looked down at the dragon, who had a mackerel in its great hot month. You could have scrambled some eggs and cooked them in his mouth.

Not far away was a building site where diggers and pneumatic drills were making the television signal in the houses go, like a red-hot pineapple volcano.

The boy looked down at his new pen knife, he had been given for his birthday. He ran up to a fisher wife, who was just walking to the supermarket to sell her wares.

Again, the squirrel looked across and saw to his delight a remarkable site. A food cart, with tropical fruit, pancakes and vindaloo flavoured pizzas.

Just below the tree, were a group of children eating sardine and stegosaurus sandwiches. The picnic was nothing remarkable, they just had juice that tasted like a new daffodil, and cakes with rosewater and honey.

And, on the blanket sat a man who was reading about his specialty of zoology and biology. This man of great knowledge had a whole archive of many wondrous books. Some old some new, but none so loved as Darwin's Evolution Arrangement.

Smells

Max stood, alert and he was twitching ready to spring at a moments notice. Roy felt the hairs on the back of his neck raise. He had been watching the wolf for over an hour.

Oh, Max knew he was there, he just tolerated this human – if he stayed far away.

Roy hurriedly wrote notes in the book – now yellow with age and use. He started as Max's nose, just moved sniffing the morning air. The damp mist was still leaving its calling card of icy droplets on everything they touched. Even the young man's hat had a droplet around its rim.

Max stood his was spring loaded. Roy knew he had to be ready to move at the speed of light, the animal would give no notice.

What Max was onto he had no idea. Roy had found the animal not far from the hut. His usual greeting of a low grumble growl, the only show of recognition.

Then Max's ears sprang up, his tail shoot into the air and the chase was on. Roy again was taken by surprise, the wolf was yards ahead, before he even moved.

He had no idea what the wolf was after? He could not hear or see anything, the mist enveloped all in its path. Roy tripped over twigs, bushes, he even slide down a slope trying to keep up. Max came to a sudden sharp halt, catching the young man off guard.

Max went flat, Roy went flat, both went along the ground like worms. Max stood again a low growl came from his throat. Slowly Roy dare lift his head. Only to find the nose of a wolf just inches away. He held his breath not daring to breath.

Roy could not forget those dark brown eyes. Pools of light showed in them. A black nose, cold and wet touched the man's face.

Then it was over. Roy was again left alone in the early morning light.

Soft white wings

As I watch the cockatoo, way up high, it reminds me of a time
long past, when people roamed this barren land.

A place where hungry people trod, upon the sun-baked land.

These people of so long ago, longing to be fed.

The snow-white bird flow up above keeping a silent watch.

As the cruel sun beats down on the sun burnt sand.

As the people cross the sand they dream of fish and bread all piled
in a basket, free to all who need, a never empty basket.

By it stands an earthen cast jar, overflowing with a rich red wine.

This again will always be a never-ending flask.

Up above the soft white wings flutter slowly down, and gently lands upon a rock.

With the soft white wings there stands a man watching all he can.

It reminds me of 2white fishes and 5 white loaves, who fed a hungry hoard.

Something was whistling

He lay under the covers; he had been that way since the lights went out. The boy was shaking like a leaf- as they say. No one could forget he was there, there was so much movement.

The young man had been on edge, ever since his lunch break. He went out the office for his break. Sitting in his usual corner in the café. He spotted a young girl at the counter looking his way. The girl smiled in a shy sort of way. He felt his face heat up when she smiled back. Then she went out, so he went back to his lunch.

Looking at his watch, it was time to get back to the office job. He paid and went out. As he was turning the corner into the square, he heard a whistle from behind. Looking around only to see the man from the café, behind him whistling this maddening tune.

He made no issue of the fact he was following him, he even smiled. He sped into his office building. As he turned to take the lift to his office standing inside the door, heading for the reception, whistling that tune. Seeing him chose a chair near the lift and sat down.

By now the man was getting fed up and he thought he would tell him to go away, if he was there when his working day had finished.

All afternoon the young man was looking at photo's, for a piece that was going into print. It was getting towards shut up shop time, and the lad heard that whistle again turning expecting to see him. Nothing was there, but still that tune echoed in his brain.

By now his head was aching with the whistle – how he wished that whistle would go away. Panic was now beginning to settle in.

The lift was on the ground floor before he realised, he had even got into the lift. The young man was in the same seat.

The man got out and went straight to the man sitting in the chair. Look here, will you stop following me, and for pity's sake stop that noise, then turned and rushed out the swinging door.

He thought that was the end of it. So, he got off the bus, and walked to his house. Only to find he had been on the bus all that time and followed him to his gate – still smiling and whistling that crazy tune.

He unlocked the door after dropping the keys and tumbling around with the lock. He rushed in and slammed the door shut and locking it from the inside. Smiling the stranger would go away now?

The man looked out the front window, he was sitting on his gate. He even waved as he made to shut his curtains.

With what now was trembling hands, he took out his mobile and rang the police. All he heard the telephone girl say. Close your curtains and lock the door. Someone would be down in the morning ......

Songs in the sky

I am lying on the ground, looking at the stars.
The sky is a curtain of blue and black,
Its jewels shinning with a silver white glow.

As I lie, they're in the still soft night.
You can hear the song of the sky.
It's a soft gentle hum, as the aroura
Spreads across the sky, red, white, blue and green.

A shooting star shoots across the jewelled night.
In that moment I hurriedly make a wish.
Then hoping that one wish will make all your dreams come true.

As you make a wish on that magic curtained sky.

Spider

Dawn was slowly making its way over the horizon. In the barn the old cockerel decided it was time to get the day going and made his way up to the frost laden roof.

Deep in the barn hidden from the suns early glare was a spider. Not a bad one, just the commonly garden variety.

With her two large hairy eyes and many long hairy legs. She had been busy through the night on her work of art.

It was an old odd pattern. Not one that an old lady would knit, on all four needles. Pick up a stich glue it to the one above, then twist a thread and attach it to the rows below.

The spider her work done, went to the middle of the row and closed her eyes. Waiting for the first move of the fine gossamer thread.

The hens were making their raucous noise, having laid their morning egg. The cockerel jumped down to put his ladies all in line.

As the day went on the far end of the barn began to warm up and the spider soaked up its warmth. Its long waiting throughout the day, but the spider did not move. No one saw the web up in the heights.

Just when the daylight began to fade, the faintest of movement was felt by the spider. Opening its eyes getting used to the dusk. Its eyes moved this way and that. With the speed of light, she made her way to the outer rim. With breakneck speed.

She began to spin a web around the unfortunate beast. That would be her midnight snack. As again her pattern of delight, she would spin in dead of night.

Stone Faces

It was an old Indian Disney movie. He could not believe what he was seeing. India was fiction, so why was the wall moving? He thought he was dreaming. So, like everyone else he pinched himself – he was awake.

First, he thought the clock was showing the wrong time. Just like Alice in Wonderland. Now this, he and his mate had been climbing up the hill for the whole afternoon. They had decided to camp beside the temple anyway.

Then rounding the bend, they came across the wall, a mighty face whose top was in the clouds.

Nothing new they just decided to climb there was a good couple of hours of daylight left and it was dry. No time like the present. So, kitted out his mated took the lead and he waited.

He felt the rock move, as he found his hand hold. Start again. This time his foot gave way, as the rock became solid.

His pal wanted to know what the holdup was, swearing, he took another hand hold. This time he rose a few feet in the air, disbelief showed on his face he was already at the cloud base. Yet he had only taken one step.

Up came his pal very cross by now. As he thought his pal had not moved.

Pulling his mate aside, he began to climb. His mate shouted he thought he was falling down. His mate looked at him rolling around on the ground. Like he was having some kind of fit.

Slowly he made his way up the rock face. He dares not look down. He could feel his pal moving. At last he stopped falling, he just lay slowly moving first one limb then another.

All the while, the rock was speaking, telling him he would not cross.

His pal had long since reached the top. He gave up on his pal below. Turned his face away and walked.

Lightning Source UK Ltd.
Milton Keynes UK
UKHW030719280921
391315UK00012B/599

9 781637 672594